Siegfried

Siegfried

by Diane Stanley · Illustrations by John Sandford

A BANTAM LITTLE ROOSTER BOOK

NEW YORK · TORONTO · LONDON · SYDNEY · AUCKLAND

For Susan Adler
with affection

—D.S.

For the Lane girl,
Patty Ann
who has loved all cats since time began:
A cat salute with upraised paw
with love from me, your brother-in-law

—J.S.

SIEGFRIED
A Bantam Little Rooster Book / October 1991

Little Rooster is a trademark of Bantam Books, a division of Bantam Doubleday Dell Publishing Group, Inc.

Library of Congress Cataloging-in-Publication Data

Stanley, Diane.
  Siegfried / by Diane Stanley: illustrated by John Sandford.
    p.   cm.
  ''A Bantam little rooster book.''
  Summary: When Mr. and Mrs. Fritz get a large and noisy cuckoo clock, their cat Siegfried decides to wage war against it.
  ISBN 0-553-07022-3
  [1. Cats—Fiction. 2. Clocks and watches—Fiction.]
I. Sandford, John, 1953–   ill. II. Title.
PZ7.S7869Si 1991
[E]—dc20   89-48768
                                                              CIP
                                                               AC

Published simultaneously in the United States and Canada

PRINTED IN HONG KONG

0 9 8 7 6 5 4 3 2

Siegfried was very old. He was, in fact, the oldest cat he knew.

In his house lived Mr. and Mrs. Fritz, who had grown old along with him and who loved him dearly. And so, living contentedly in his cozy world, Siegfried was not at all prepared for the dark cloud that would soon overshadow his happiness.

It was Christmas. The Fritzes'
children, Elizabeth and Ryan,
who were all grown up and lived
in their own houses, had come
to visit. They had brought plenty
of presents to put under the tree.
Elizabeth's gift—the very large one
marked "Handle with Care"—was
the cause of what happened to
Siegfried.

The mysterious present turned
out to be a most peculiar clock,
which had come all the way from
Germany. It was shaped like a tiny
house with an arched door.
Pinecones hung on chains from its
bottom. Siegfried had never seen
anything like it.

Mr. Fritz hung the clock on the living-room wall and pulled the chains so that the pinecones were drawn up to the bottom of the house. This started the clock ticking. Then the family went into the kitchen to see if the turkey had started to brown and to begin work on the sweet potatoes, peas, and cranberry sauce. Siegfried curled up for a nap.

He had drifted into a most peaceful sleep when, suddenly, the clock went *BONG! BONG!*

Siegfried sprang from his seat.
Then the clock's door opened and
out popped a little yellow bird.
"Cuckoo, cuckoo!" said the bird.
Then it went back inside the clock.

Siegfried stared as the door
snapped shut. "I am *not* a
cuckoo!" he hissed. "Who does
this bird think it is, coming into
my house and ringing bells when
I'm asleep—and calling me names!"

As he thought about it some
more, he muttered, "Who, indeed!"

Siegfried paced the floor, watching the clock. Nothing happened. "You're afraid to try that funny stuff when I'm awake," he grumbled. There was no answer. All he heard was the *tick-tock* of the clock and the sound of Mr. Fritz setting the table in the dining room.

Siegfried continued to pace during dinner. Ordinarily he would have been in the dining room, weaving among the chairs and the feet, looking for tidbits that had fallen to the floor. But this Christmas dinner he stayed in the living room, keeping a sharp eye out for the bird.

The more he thought about it, the angrier he became. Finally, filled to the brim with rage and frustration, Siegfried heaved himself onto the mantel, leaned over the edge, and uttered threats directly into the face of the clock.

"I dare you to come out!" he challenged.

BONG! BONG! BONG! went the clock.

With a scream, Siegfried shot straight up, then dropped to the floor with a thud. He looked up just in time for the bird's second appearance.

"Cuckoo, cuckoo!" said the bird.

Siegfried lunged. "Cuckoo!" added the bird, disappearing just in time for the door to snap shut on Siegfried's nose.

"I'm going to get you . . . you, you . . . bird!" swore Siegfried, rubbing his injured nose on the satin sofa.

As afternoon faded into evening he watched the clock, waiting for the bird. He was too nervous to eat his Kitty Pretty when Mrs. Fritz called him. He showed no interest in the catnip from his stocking. When the family went for a ride in the car, he refused to go along.

"Do you think Siegfried is sick?" asked Elizabeth.

"Just too much excitement," was Mr. Fritz's opinion.

Siegfried was sure that his life would be miserable as long as that bird was living in his house. He paced in circles on the living-room carpet, thinking dark thoughts. The clock's loud *BONG*s went through him like electric shocks. Siegfried was a wreck.

When it got dark, the family
came back and ate leftovers in the
kitchen. Siegfried went to another
part of the house to get some rest.
Instead, he had a nightmare . . .

Siegfried awoke feeling heartsick. He was tired and his head ached. But he was also filled with a new determination. He was going to win the war and show the newcomer once and for all *whose house this was.*

Siegfried returned to the field of battle. The ticking of the clock seemed unnaturally loud in the morning quiet. He sat in the middle of the room and stared at the clock. It was then that he noticed something about the hands on the clock. They moved—very, very slowly. When the big hand pointed to the ceiling, the bird appeared. And that is how, in a manner of speaking, Siegfried learned to tell time.

He watched for several hours,
just to make sure. By the time the
family came downstairs, he was

ready for his Kitty Pretty. Siegfried
had figured out the bird's secret.
And now he was ready to teach it
a thing or two.

He returned to the living room
and began to make practice leaps
from the chair to the mantel, from
the card table to the china
cupboard.

He watched and waited. And then, at about the time Siegfried usually took his morning nap on the window seat, the big hand reached the top of the clock. *BONG! BONG! BONG! BONG! BONG! BONG! BONG! BONG! BONG!* went the clock. Out came the enemy.

Siegfried was not on the window seat. He was crouched and ready.

He was in the air. He caught the bird and, for one brief moment, held it between his teeth .

CRASH! Siegfried, the bird, and the clock fell in a tangled heap onto the floor. The bird lay on the rug. The clock lay mostly on top of Siegfried. The clock didn't make a sound.

The entire Fritz family came running from the kitchen to see what had happened.

"Poor Siegfried!" Elizabeth cried.

"How on earth did the clock fall on you?" cooed Mrs. Fritz as she checked him for injuries.

"What a mess!" said Mr. Fritz.

For the rest of the morning the family fussed over Siegfried—everyone but Mr. Fritz, who was busy at the kitchen table trying to put the clock back together. At last he had done all he could for it—or at least all he was going to do. He hung the clock back up on the living-room wall, this time using two strong nails, just to be sure.

The house grew quiet as the family napped or read their new Christmas books. Siegfried settled onto the window seat, in full view of the clock. He wondered whether the bird would dare—after such a beating—to come out and call him names again. The suspense was terrible.

At last the hour arrived.

CLICK! CLICK! went the clock.

"Well, that's better," mused Siegfried.

The door opened. The bird came out, somewhat crooked on its little spring.

"Whirrrr, whirrrr!" it said. Then it hobbled back inside, and the door squeaked shut.